Cute and Cuddly: Baby Animals

BUNNIES

By Grace Elora

Please visit our Web site, www.garethstevens.com. For a free color catalog of all our high-quality books, call toll free 1-800-542-2595 or fax 1-877-542-2596.

Library of Congress Cataloging-in-Publication Data

Elora, Grace.
  Bunnies / Grace Elora.
    p. cm. — (Cute and cuddly—baby animals)
  ISBN 978-1-4339-4503-8 (library binding)
  ISBN 978-1-4339-4504-5 (pbk.)
  ISBN 978-1-4339-4505-2 (6-pack)
  1. Rabbits—Infancy—Juvenile literature. I. Title.
  QL737.L32E46 2011
  599.32'139—dc22
                                        2010032881

First Edition

Published in 2011 by
Gareth Stevens Publishing
111 East 14th Street, Suite 349
New York, NY 10003

Copyright © 2011 Gareth Stevens Publishing

Editor: Therese Shea
Designer: Andrea Davison-Bartolotta

Photo credits: Cover, pp. 1, 3, 5, 7, 9, 11, 13, 15, 19, 21, 23, 24 (tail) Shutterstock.com; pp. 17, 24 (fur) Duncan Usher/Foto Natura/Minden Pictures/Getty Images.

All rights reserved. No part of this book may be reproduced in any form without permission in writing from the publisher, except by a reviewer.

Printed in the United States of America

CPSIA compliance information: Batch #CW11GS: For further information contact Gareth Stevens, New York, New York at 1-800-542-2595.

BUNNIES

Baby rabbits are bunnies.

Bunnies live in holes in the ground.

Bunnies have no fur at first. Fur grows after a few days.

Some bunnies have white tails. They are called cottontails.

Bunnies have long ears.
They can hear danger.

Bunnies sleep during the day.

Bunnies play and eat at night.

Bunnies eat grass. They eat other plants, too.

Bunnies have long back legs. They use them to hop.

Bunnies hop on their toes!

Words to Know

fur

tail

Sayville Library
88 Greene Avenue
Sayville, NY 11782

SEP 13 2011

DISCARDED BY
SAYVILLE LIBRARY